ALOLAN CHALLENGE

Adapted by Jeanette Lane

ORCHARD

ORCHARD BOOKS

First published in the USA by Scholastic Inc in 2018
First published in the UK in 2018 by The Watts Publishing Group
This edition published in 2018

3 5 7 9 10 8 6 4

A CIP catalogue record for this book is available from the British Library.

ISBN 978 1 40835 730 9

Printed and bound in Great Britain

The paper and board used in this book are
made from wood from responsible sources.

Orchard Books
An imprint of Hachette Children's Group
Part of The Watts Publishing Group Limited
Carmelite House, 50 Victoria Embankment, London EC4Y 0DZ

An Hachette UK Company

www.hachette.co.uk
www.hachettechildrens.co.uk

CHAPTER 1

A NEW POKÉMON

For ten-year-old Ash Ketchum, every day was a step on his grand journey to becoming a Pokémon Master. Since he'd arrived in the Alola region, Ash had enrolled in the Pokémon School, where he and Pikachu had met many new friends and Pokémon. Each and every day, they were learning new things and having exciting adventures.

Ash and Pikachu loved exploring Alola. One of Ash's favourite parts of being in a new place was discovering all the new Pokémon. Since they'd first come to Alola, they'd met many new Pokémon friends and they'd also found a new battling partner for their team. The adorable Rowlet was a Grass- and Flying-type Pokémon with a knack for sneaking up on opponents … and then sleeping away the rest of the day in Ash's backpack!

One morning, Ash was on his way to school when he encountered a Pokémon he hadn't seen before. It stared at him with its intense yellow eyes. Ash stared right back.

In no time, Rotom Dex gave Ash the lowdown on the Pokémon. "Litten. The Fire Cat Pokémon," Rotom Dex announced,

hovering in the air just behind Ash.
"A Fire-type. Litten show few emotions
and prefer being alone."

Rotom Dex was a unique companion
for Ash. Rotom was a Pokémon that had
the ability to live inside various electronic
devices. This Rotom was a present from
Ash's teacher, Professor Kukui. Rotom had

slipped straight from a plug socket and into a Pokédex. Now it was an amazing talking device that kept Ash informed about all the unknown Pokémon in Alola. Ash took Rotom Dex with him almost everywhere.

Litten stood on top of a stone wall and kept its steely eyes on Ash. Ash knelt down, trying to lure it his way.

"Litten takes time to build any level of trust," Rotom Dex told Ash.

Ash heard Rotom, but he still wanted to try to make friends with the cute Litten.

Litten jumped down from the wall and approached Ash.

"Hi. What's up?" Ash said, holding out his hand.

Without hesitating, Litten began to rub up against Ash's knees. Pikachu watched from its perch on Ash's shoulder.

"Hey, maybe you're hungry!" Ash said. He opened his backpack and pulled something out. "See? It's my lunch," he explained to the curious Litten.

Ash was excited about the lunch that Professor Kukui had prepared for him. The professor was not only Ash's teacher, but he was also his host. Ash was staying with the professor in his cosy island bungalow for the school year. Professor Kukui was an expert on Pokémon and he could also make a delicious sandwich.

"Yay! Yummy," Ash said. He tore off a corner of the sandwich and offered it to Litten. "Here you go. It's great!"

"Mrow? Mrow?" Litten looked at the corner of the sandwich in Ash's one hand and then it looked at the larger part of the sandwich in Ash's other hand. All at once, it leapt for the larger chunk of sandwich, swiping it right out of Ash's hand. Litten tried to escape, but not before Ash grabbed its thick tail.

Litten lashed out with its claws, hitting Ash across the face. Rotom Dex chased it down, but Litten swatted Rotom away with a brisk

swish of its tail. Ash, Pikachu and
Rotom Dex watched as Litten trotted off
along the stone wall, jumped down and
escaped out of sight.

What a way to start the morning. Now Ash
was running late for school.

The Pokémon School was on the island
of Melemele, which was one of many
beautiful tropical islands in the region.
Ash had originally visited Melemele on
holiday with his mum. With its strong sun,
lush forests, long stretches of beach and
fresh, delicious food, the entire Alola
region was a paradise.

Of course, Ash didn't feel like Melemele
was paradise that morning. He was really
annoyed about his encounter with Litten.
It wasn't just that he'd lost his lunch.
Ash sensed something else in Litten

and he wasn't sure what it was. He hoped
his friends at school might be able to
fill him in.

CHAPTER 2

LOOKING
FOR
LITTEN

"Wow, so you finally met that Litten," Mallow said. She was standing by the balcony in their classroom. As she looked out over the ocean, the breeze blew through her long green ponytails.

"Is it your friend?" Ash questioned.

"Litten comes up asking for food all the time," Mallow explained. "It's so cute!"

"I fall for it every time!" Lana added. Both Bounsweet and Popplio, Mallow's and Lana's Pokémon, cooed in agreement.

Ash liked Mallow and Lana. He trusted their opinions, but he didn't feel the same way about Litten.

"Well, I don't think it's so cute," Ash said.

"That's how I lost most of my sandwich!"

"You mean Litten stole it?" Lillie asked.

"You got it," Ash replied.

Ash's classmates laughed and groaned. They weren't making fun of Ash. They felt bad for him, but the story was quite funny.

"That sounds like our Litten, all right," Lana said.

"Litten's not the kind who enjoys dealing with people," added Sophocles, another classmate. "It takes a long time to warm up to Trainers, too. They say it's not your average Pokémon."

"That's precisely what I told Ash earlier," Rotom Dex declared.

"You could say Litten's the lone star of Pokémon, right?" said Mallow. "It always seems to be hanging around our restaurant."

"I see it in the market, too," Kiawe said. "It steals all kinds of berries."

"Still, Litten is so cute. I just can't get angry at it," Mallow shrugged.

Kiawe, who was the oldest of the students in the class, seemed less enchanted by Litten than the others. He also seemed to understand Ash's frustration. "So, do you have a plan?" he asked Ash. "To deal with Litten?"

"Someone should teach it!" Ash insisted. "You don't mess with a guy's sandwich!"

"Wait. Teach it?" Lillie asked. "What are you talking about?"

Lillie was the one student who didn't have her own Pokémon. She enjoyed researching Pokémon more than training them.

"I know just what to do," Ash said with certainty. "I'll catch it!"

All of Ash's classmates were surprised. After everything they had told him about Litten, Ash still seemed to think he could get the stubborn, independent Pokémon to join his team.

The next day, Professor Kukui and Ash were shopping at the local outdoor market. They had already bought lots of fresh fruit and vegetables for dinner. The teacher was listing the things they still needed to find when, like a flash, Litten ran by.

Just as quick, Ash and Pikachu were on its tail.

"A Litten sighting!" cried Rotom Dex. It began explaining the situation to Professor Kukui.

Litten was quick … and sneaky. After racing past several fruit stands, Ash and

Pikachu had lost track of the little Litten. Where could it have gone?

"Want to buy some berries, dear?" a kind woman asked Ash. She had grey hair and glasses with thin wire frames.

Ash quickly turned her down. "No, we were looking for a Litten." He scanned the area. "There it is!" he exclaimed, locating Litten just inside the woman's fruit stand.

To no one's surprise, it was eating.

As soon as Litten saw Ash, it raised its head and growled. Ash clenched his teeth.

"Now you two," the shopkeeper said, "let's play nice."

"You give it food?" Ash questioned.

"In Alola, nature's bounty is for sharing," the woman said. She bent over and handed Litten a big, juicy berry. "Now, dear, don't eat too fast. I love to feed you, Litten."

Litten looked very content. It trotted off with the berry in its mouth.

By this time, Professor Kukui had caught up to the others. "Does that Litten come here a lot?" he asked the woman.

"All the time," she responded. "A habit, every day. Honestly, I think Litten enjoys looking out for me. That's why I have berries waiting when it comes by for a visit."

"Now, let me guess," she said, turning to Ash, "Litten made off with some of your food, didn't it?"

"It sure did!" Ash replied. "My sandwich, specially made!" He felt frustrated all over again. If Litten had eaten his sandwich, why was it still so hungry? Why did it need a bowl of fruit and a big berry, too? And why did so many people like to care for it when

it wasn't very nice to them?

"Ash," Professor Kukui said, "I can make you another one." Like Ash's classmates, his teacher wasn't certain why Ash was so upset.

The shopkeeper laughed to herself. "I have no idea where Litten lives, but it certainly is a dear."

CHAPTER 3

LITTEN IN TROUBLE

The next afternoon, Ash, Pikachu, and
Rotom Dex said goodbye to their friends
at school and headed for home. They took
their usual winding path on a road that
looked out over the sea. Melemele Island
was so peaceful!

At least, it was usually peaceful. Ash heard

some kind of commotion on the hill below. When Ash peeked over the fence on the side of the road, he saw Litten! It was facing off with a much larger Pokémon.

"Rotom, who's that Pokémon?" Ash called out.

"It's a Persian," Rotom Dex responded.

"Persian? It's not like any Persian I've ever seen," Ash replied. Ash had learned that

some of the local Pokémon had adapted to look very different from the versions that Ash knew from Kanto. Ash was familiar with a tan-coloured Persian with a red jewel on its head. The Alolan version was grey and the gem on its forehead was turquoise. They really did look different.

"The Alolan Persian is a Dark-type, so it can be cunning with a bit of a mean streak," Rotom warned.

"But that means that … it's gonna …" Ash's voice trailed off as he watched the action below with concern.

Persian was advancing toward Litten. Litten was backing away, but it was nearing a steep cliff. Below the cliff, there was only ocean. Litten held a yellow berry in its mouth.

"Rrrrrraa! Rrrrrraa!" Persian took a step

forward, menacing Litten. Then, all at once, Persian used Fury Swipes, knocking Litten clear off its feet.

"Don't do that!" Ash yelled as he skidded down the rocky hillside. Pikachu was right at his side. "This has gotta stop! Knock it off!" he scolded Persian. "For a single berry, you're being way too rough."

"Pika!" Pikachu agreed.

Annoyed, Persian aimed a Power Gem move at them.

Litten tried to pick up its berry and slip away, but Persian wasn't done with the Fire Cat Pokémon.

"Rrrrrraa. Rrrrrraa!" Persian had Litten trapped at the edge of the cliff!

"I said knock it off!" Ash shouted. "Pikachu, Electro Ball!"

Pikachu threw an Electro Ball. Persian dodged it. But it was not as lucky when Ash ordered a Thunderbolt attack. Pikachu's blast landed with a ZAP! Persian finally got the message and skulked away.

Ash, Pikachu, and Rotom turned their attention to Litten, who was limping away.

"Hey, Litten," Ash said. "Are you okay?"

"Litten has taken a lot of damage," Rotom Dex said.

It worried Ash to see Litten in pain. "Don't push yourself so hard!" Ash advised. "C'mon, please!"

Pikachu begged Litten, too, but the Pokémon was too stubborn to listen.

Ash walked towards Litten. He knew that the Pokémon was injured and he wanted to help. At least he could carry the berry for the hurt Pokémon.

But when Ash reached out for the yellow fruit, Litten nipped at him. "Litten? Let's work together," Ash suggested. "We're going to the Pokémon Center."

Litten didn't like that idea one bit. It wrestled away from Ash's hands.

Pikachu tried to convince Litten, but it wasn't until the exhausted Pokémon nearly passed out that Ash could grab hold of it.

Ash promised Litten that he wasn't trying

to take the berry away. It was just that Litten
needed help so it could recover from its
battle.

With Litten still struggling, Ash carried
it off. "Rotom, grab Litten's berry!" he
instructed. And to Litten he demanded,
"Stop biting me!"

At the Pokémon Center, Nurse Joy did her
best to bandage Litten so the injuries would

heal properly. She wrapped a bandage around its back and belly several times. Still, she was worried that Litten would try to lick its wounds, so she put a Heliolisk Collar around its neck. The collar looked like a big disk that shielded its head. Litten was not happy about it.

Once she was finished with Litten, Nurse Joy told Ash that it was his turn. "Litten's not the only one who got hurt," she pointed out. Ash looked down and realised he had scratches up and down his arms.

As they prepared to clean up Ash's cuts, Litten sneakily snatched the berry and leapt from its bed.

"Hey, stop!" yelled Ash. He raced after Litten.

"Ash, try to make sure Litten doesn't overdo it!" Nurse Joy called out.

On the way out the door, Ash passed Kiawe.

Kiawe shook his head as he stared after his classmate. "All that for a sandwich," Kiawe murmured.

But for Ash, this was way beyond a sandwich now.

CHAPTER 4

STOUTLAND SURPRISE

Ash had almost caught up with Litten when
the feisty Pokémon tried to jump through
an iron fence. But Litten couldn't fit
through the bars because of its bulky collar.
The dazed Pokémon fell backwards onto
the pavement.

Ash stared down at it. "Will you listen to

me, please?" he begged. "From now on, no running away! You're not doing what you're told and it's only hurting you."

Ash scooped up the little Pokémon. He had no choice: he had to take Litten to Professor Kukui's place.

The professor was understanding, as long as it was just for the night. Litten seemed willing to take it easy there. Ash even removed the collar so Litten could relax and the independent Pokémon curled up and fell fast asleep in Ash's lap.

Ash sighed. He wished Litten would trust him more.

Many hours later, Ash blinked his bleary eyes open. It was still the middle of the night and he'd been sound asleep. He heard a scratching. He got up and noticed Litten standing by the door. "Yeah, yeah. I'll open it in a second."

It wasn't until Litten had already bolted out the open door that Ash really woke up and realised what had happened. Yikes!

"Where's Litten going?" he yelled, rousing Rotom Dex.

"Data is incomplete!" Rotom Dex replied. "Litten's full recovery requires lots of sleep and the absence of stress and strain!"

In no time, Ash, Pikachu and Rotom Dex

were chasing Litten again. They ran down city streets until they came to a remote lane that led to an old, deserted, ivy-covered cottage. Litten ran inside.

Ash, Pikachu and Rotom all crept inside after it. They saw Litten run to the back room. There, Litten dropped the yellow berry on a table.

"A Stoutland," Ash mumbled, seeing the large Pokémon resting on a couch.

"One that's getting on in years, I'd say," added Rotom.

"I wonder if Litten's been stealing food to bring to Stoutland," Ash thought out loud. That was why Litten needed so much food!

When Litten realised they were there, it turned to face them and hissed. It was clearly protecting the older Stoutland. Ash guessed that the Stoutland had once protected Litten when it was tiny.

As Stoutland munched on the berry, Pikachu reassured Litten that they were there to help.

Ash knelt down next to the two Pokémon. "Guess your dinner's a little late. Sorry, Stoutland," he said softly. "See, Litten got hurt in a fight, so we all went to my place to rest."

Ash took a deep breath and turned to Litten. "Litten, I was hoping I could catch you so you'd be on my team. But now that I see what you're doing, it was a bad plan."

Ash really admired Litten's devotion to its friend. He was glad that he could finally understand why Litten acted the way it did.

Ash looked at Pikachu and Rotom. "We'd better head home. Professor Kukui might get worried," he said. "And next time I visit,

I'll bring some food for you." This time, he was talking to Litten. "I can come visit, can't I?"

Just then, they all heard a sound come from outside.

"It appears something is approaching!" Rotom warned them.

"What is it?" Ash asked.

The Alolan Persian leapt down from a high window and aimed its turquoise gem at them.

"Quick! Let's get outside!" Ash declared. He, Pikachu, Rotom Dex, and Litten all dashed out the door as Persian sent a blast their way.

Persian pounced and landed right in front of Litten and Pikachu. "Such persistence! There's no doubt Persian is out for revenge," Rotom observed.

Pikachu and Litten bounded forward, ready to defend their friends. "Take it easy," Ash advised them. "Why don't you give it up?" he asked Persian.

Persian growled in response.

Ash called for a Thunderbolt attack. Pikachu aimed and Litten got ready for its Ember move. But Persian was too quick and attacked Ash with Fury Swipes!

Litten looked concerned but Ash brushed it off. "A few scratches aren't going to hurt me!"

Persian came at Pikachu and Litten again. Stoutland began to murmur instructions to Litten. It was giving the younger Pokémon battle advice! Litten listened closely.

Litten focused its energy. The bandages wrapped around its belly burst off and Litten's whole body seemed to pulse with

fiery power. Litten faced Persian and blasted a huge cough of fire for its mightiest Ember ever!

The fireball struck Persian head-on and the Classy Cat Pokémon raced off, its tail still smoking.

Stoutland gave a gruff huff of approval and Ash cheered. "That was awesome, Litten!"

Litten gave Ash a little smile. Then it

trotted over to Stoutland and the older Pokémon looked proud.

"I detect a happy ending," Rotom Dex announced. "Except for you not catching Litten …"

But Ash still felt it was a happy ending. He and Litten had an understanding.

The next day, Ash was in for a surprise. He, Pikachu, and Rotom Dex stopped by the ivy-covered cottage to drop off food for Litten and Stoutland. They had two full bags to share, but Litten and Stoutland weren't there.

Where could they have gone? Ash assumed that he must have done something wrong.

Worried, Ash decided to visit the shopkeeper who was friends with Litten. "I feel like it's my fault," he told her.

The woman studied Ash through her wire-framed glasses. "Pokémon are Pokémon, and people are people," she said. "One being's world isn't exactly the same as the other's. So don't go blaming yourself. Litten's living under the same Alolan sky as you."

Ash thought about her advice. He supposed he needed to try to see things from Litten's point of view. He wondered if their paths would cross again.

Just then, a stealthy black Pokémon with familiar red markings appeared at the shopkeeper's fruit stand. "Litten!" the woman said. "I heard you moved."

Litten looked surprised to see Ash and Pikachu there. Had the three become friends, or was Litten still set on standing alone?

Only time would tell, but it was clear that Ash had learned an important lesson about allowing Pokémon to be Pokémon. It was yet another step on his long journey to become a Pokémon Master.

CHAPTER 5

QUEST FOR A Z-CRYSTAL

"Huh?" Rotom Dex was confused. It was a school morning and Rotom was ready to pester Ash until he finally got out of bed but Ash was already awake. "What have you done with the Ash who sleeps late?" the device asked.

"I can't wait until I can use a Z-Move

again!" Ash announced from his bed. "Which means I'm gonna have to get myself a Z-Crystal." He got up and put on his clothes.

After Ash's experience with Litten, he had decided to focus on his original goal for his time in the Alola region. He wanted to earn another Z-Crystal so he and Pikachu could master their very own Z-Move.

Ever since he had seen Kiawe and Charizard do their Z-Move, Ash had been fascinated by the special skill. To do a Z-Move, a Pokémon Trainer needed to possess a Z-Ring, which was a kind of bracelet that Trainers usually earned only through a set of complicated tasks called the Island Challenge.

To Ash's surprise – and that of all his classmates at the Pokémon School – Ash had received a Z-Ring from the Island Guardian named Tapu Koko. No one knew why the mysterious Legendary Pokémon had given him a Z-Ring. The Z-Ring already had a powerful Z-Crystal inside.

It was an awesome, unexpected gift, but the Z-Crystal had exploded after Ash's first attempt to do the special Z-Move. Oddly enough, the crystal had shattered during Ash's first battle with Tapu Koko.

Now Ash needed to earn another one. He and Pikachu were ready to do whatever it took to take this next step on their journey together.

At breakfast, Ash shared his plan with Professor Kukui.

"A Z-Crystal?" his teacher asked.

"Yeah," Ash confirmed. "I want to get a lot stronger and then have a rematch with

Tapu Koko." In his mind, he pictured Tapu Koko. The Island Guardian was yellow, with a big orange crest on its head, wide wings and bold markings that made it look like a warrior. "I can't wait to try those Z-Moves again. Right, buddy?"

"Pika, pika!" Pikachu was in full agreement.

"You're as fired up as if you were hit by a Blast Burn!" commented Professor Kukui.

Ash nodded as he took a bite of breakfast. "I remember Kiawe saying that you can earn Z-Crystals by going through the Island Challenge."

"Well, that isn't the only way, but it is the most certain way," Ash's teacher said. He seemed pretty excited about the topic, too. "The key to success is passing the grand trial of each of the islands' kahunas."

Ash gulped down some milk. "So how do you do that?" he asked.

Rotom Dex nudged his way in front of Professor Kukui. "I will answer that with pleasure! A grand trial is a battle between the Trainer and the island kahuna. If the Trainer wins, the kahuna acknowledges the Trainer's worthiness."

"Whoa," Ash said. "Sounds like fun!"

"Fun?" the professor questioned, pushing

Rotom aside. "You're up against a kahuna, so if you're overconfident, you can get yourself hurt! And …"

"According to my data," Rotom interrupted, "a grand trial is preceded by lesser trials that must be overcome first."

"Got it. First some little trials, then BOOM!" cried Ash.

"All right, all right," Professor Kukui said, seeing Ash's enthusiasm. "I think we should go pay a visit to Hala. He is the kahuna of Melemele Island."

"Right!" Ash cheered.

"Pika! Pika!" Pikachu exclaimed.

Soon Professor Kukui, Ash, Pikachu and Rotom were on their way. Little did they know that there was trouble brewing close by. A pack of Rattata and Raticate had devoured a whole crop of Pinap Berries.

When the farmer and his dog came out to chase the pesky Pokémon away, the pack scampered out of the field and started to stampede across a nearby street. Then the Rattata and Raticate ran right in front of three Tauros who were pulling a heavy load on a trailer. The Tauros had to stop so fast, their cargo of lumber toppled over and blocked the entire road.

When Ash and the others came across the scene, they had no idea what had happened. "What's going on?" Ash wondered.

"I'd say it was an accident," Rotom Dex replied.

"Attention!" Officer Jenny called out. "This road will be closed until the timber can be removed. Until that happens, please use a different route."

Ash frowned. He wondered what could
have caused the accident. It was frustrating.
He didn't want any delays in his new plan to
earn a Z-Crystal. Why did there have to be
an accident on this road, on today of
all days?

Professor Kukui approached Officer Jenny
and asked if she could tell them what had
happened. The officer recognised him
at once.

"Professor Kukui!" she said. She then explained that the whole problem was the fault of the menacing Rattata and Raticate. Ash was amazed that Pokémon could be responsible for such a mess.

"Are you a student at the Pokémon School?" Officer Jenny asked.

"Yeah, my name's Ash," he replied.

"Pika! Pika!" Pikachu put in.

"This is my partner, Pikachu and Rotom Dex," Ash continued.

"I'm Officer Jenny. Glad to be at your service." She raised her hand to her head in a salute. "Actually, I'm a graduate of the Pokémon School, too."

Ash's face lit up. "Wow! That's so cool!" he exclaimed. Then the excitement of the crowd distracted him. Everyone was in awe of a massive Pokémon's strength as it helped move the timber off the road and back onto the trailer. It was Hariyama. Ash hurried toward it. "You're so strong! Those logs are like twigs to you!"

Ash was amazed to see a man lift one of the logs. He had a broad white mustache and white hair that was pulled in a ponytail on the back of his head. The man wore a yellow robe with wide sleeves and a white belt tied in a large knot at his waist.

"This gentleman is Hala," Professor Kukui told Ash. "He is the island kahuna."

CHAPTER 6

ALOLA ISLAND KAHUNA

"Thanks a lot, Kahuna Hala," Officer Jenny said.

"Of course," the man responded. "It's my job to solve any problems thc island may encounter."

Ash stared in amazement. This man was the island kahuna? And he was there to help with the accident that had stopped Ash and Professor Kukui? Could it really be a coincidence?

"I have a clean up crew on their way here now," Officer Jenny assured the kahuna, pointing to a pickup truck. "And there they are."

A group of four Machamp jumped from the back of the truck. They immediately formed an assembly line. Each Machamp

used all four arms to pass two logs at a time. It took only a few minutes for them to load all the logs back on the trailer.

"Thank you all for your cooperation," Officer Jenny called out to the crowd.

Ash took the chance to talk directly to the kahuna. He wanted to let him know of his plans. "I'm actually here for the Island Challenge," Ash explained.

"I'm well aware of that," Kahuna Hala replied. "I've been waiting," the older man continued, "so why don't you and the professor come by sometime soon?"

"We certainly will, sir!" Professor Kukui assured him.

The very next day, Ash and Professor Kukui showed up at Kahuna Hala's home.

"Oh, that was fast," Hala said when he

answered the door. "Please come in." He gave Professor Kukui, Ash, Pikachu and Rotom Dex a tour of his home. When they passed his office, Ash noticed a shelf where several Z-Rings were displayed.

Hala noted that Ash had eyed the powerful rings. "Yes," he confirmed. "The Z-Ring you are now wearing is one that I made."

Ash was shocked. He had not realised that Kahuna Hala crafted Z-Rings. "You made it?" he questioned. "But I got it from Tapu Koko."

Hala nodded solemnly. "I thought that might be the case. One day, I noticed that one of my Z-Rings could not be accounted for," he explained. "Then I realised it was the work of Tapu Koko."

"Has something like that ever happened

before?" Ash's teacher asked, curious.

"This is the first time Tapu Koko's ever taken a Z-Ring, that's for sure," Hala answered with certainty. "It appears Tapu Koko has a strong interest in you, young man."

"Huh?" Ash was confused by Kahuna Hala's comment.

"I'm just talking to myself," the kahuna responded. By this time, they had all settled down on the comfortable sofas in the kahuna's living room. The kahuna's Hariyama joined them.

Ash decided it was time to get down to business. "Kahuna, I'd like to get a Z-Crystal as soon as I can. I'll need it for when I battle Tapu Koko again."

"Again?" Hala repeated. He paused for a moment. "Ash, if you don't mind, I'd like you to answer a question for me."

"A question? For me?" Ash wondered what the older man meant.

"I assume you now know that the people of this island have been troubled by a rash of wild Rattata and Raticate. Am I right?"

"Yes, sir," Ash answered.

"If you were the person being asked to solve this problem," Hala continued, "what would you do?"

Ash couldn't answer right away. Professor Kukui chuckled to himself, as if he knew that the kahuna would expect Ash to tackle this kind of challenge.

"I know!" Ash declared. "I'd take Pikachu and Rowlet and challenge them all to a battle, then ..."

"My young Ash," Hala interrupted. "Are you interested in learning why the Island

Challenge was started so many years ago? You see, it wasn't simply to make Trainers stronger in battle. It was to raise young people in such a way that they will love and protect the islands of Alola as well as the many people and Pokémon who inhabit them."

What Kahuna Hala said made Ash thoughtful. "Love all that's here and protect it," Ash murmured. Pikachu curled up on Ash's lap.

Hala looked seriously at Ash. "I want you to look for answers that won't only lead to battle. We'll talk about the Z-Crystal after I've heard what you come up with."

Ash closed his eyes and put his arms behind his head. He tried to figure out the Rattata and Raticate problem.

"During my trial," Professor Kukui shared, "I spent quite a long time thinking about Hala's question, too."

"During your trial?" Ash asked.

"Yeah," Professor Kukui confirmed.

Kahuna Hala laughed at that. He knew Ash must be surprised that he had also been in charge of the Island Challenge for Ash's teacher. "Food for thought, huh?" Hala smiled. "Instead of rushing through things and answering right away, why not take your time and think it over?"

Ash sighed and thought about Hala's question some more.

The next day at Pokémon School, Ash was still thinking. In fact, he was thinking so much that his classmates were amazed.

"Ash has been thinking about something for that long?" Mallow said. Her Pokémon partner, Bounsweet, was sitting on her shoulder.

"Incredible," Lana commented.

Ash had his head down on his desk, and he was moaning in pain – the pain of thinking especially hard.

Finally, Kiawe couldn't take it anymore. "All right, please just tell us what Kahuna Hala said."

Ash's head was still down and his eyes were closed. He looked depressed.

Kiawe sighed. "We may even be able to help you."

Ash's eyes popped open.

"All you have to do is let us know what he said," Lillie assured him.

Ash told them everything he knew about the Rattata and Raticate and he explained that his solution could not include a traditional Pokémon battle.

Lillie, who loved to research, suggested they learn more about Rattata and Raticate. "That information might give us a clue," she offered.

"I believe that's my cue," Rotom said, swooshing in. Ash grabbed hold of the device so he could see the screen better. His classmates gathered around his desk.

Ash was surprised to see the differences in the Alolan form of the long-toothed

Pokémon. Somehow, the Alolan forms of these Mouse Pokémon seemed more menacing and fierce.

"Rattata and its evolved form, Raticate," Rotom Dex began. "The Mouse Pokémon. A Dark- and Normal-type. When they band together, Rattata and Raticate steal food from people's homes. Long ago, they came here to the Alolan islands aboard cargo ships and eventually grew into the Pokémon we see today. The numbers of Rattata and Raticate grew so large that Yungoos and Gumshoos were brought in from a different region to chase them off."

"That's it!" the group of friends cheered.

CHAPTER 7

GO, PIKACHU!

"I see," Kahuna Hala said to Ash when he visited the very next day. "You're saying if we ask Yungoos and Gumshoos to help us, we can all solve the problem together?"

"Yes, sir!" Ash responded.

"Now, that's a thoughtful and wise answer. It's my answer, too."

"All right!" Ash exclaimed. He wondered what would happen next.

"Now, I must be honest and tell you my question was to test whether you had what it takes to go through the actual trial itself," Hala explained.

Ash was surprised to hear that. "Then I should be honest and let you know that I found the answer together with all of my friends," he confessed. "I hope that wasn't wrong."

"No, not at all," Kahuna Hala responded. "When we are searching for life's answers, we should always look to our friends for help. That in itself is a very important life lesson!"

Ash breathed a sigh of relief.

"Then, shall we go?" Hala asked. He stood up and led Ash out the door.

They soon arrived at the mouth of a great cave. Kahuna Hala paused in front of the cave and informed Ash of the plan, which had several stages. "There are many Yungoos and Gumshoos living in this cave," he explained. "They are all very strong, but there is one Gumshoos who is so amazingly powerful. It is called the Totem Pokémon."

"Totem Pokémon?" Ash repeated.

"Yes. There are several Pokémon in Alola who have that name. Most of them are following the lead of the Island Guardians, as they assist Trainers who undertake the Island Challenge." Hala peered at Ash to see if the young Trainer was following his explanation. "So, Ash, your trial is to take on the Totem Pokémon in a Pokémon battle and be victorious. Then, if you succeed, I want you to chase away the Rattata and Raticate with the aid of the Totem Pokémon."

As soon as he finished, Kahuna Hala stepped into the moss-lined tunnel that led to the cave.

"But wait," Ash said, running to catch up. "Why would Gumshoos team up with me?"

"Never fear!" Hala said, striding ahead. "If

you can earn the Totem Pokémon's respect during your battle challenge, it will assist you in your time of need." They stepped into a giant cavern. "I will be watching. I will be the referee during your trial."

Ash looked around at the great space. Lush plants grew down the walls of red rock. There were several tunnels that led deeper into the hillside. Misty sunlight streamed in through two openings in the cave ceiling.

"It's huge," Ash said under his breath. For the first time, he wondered if he was prepared for this challenge.

"Totem Pokémon Gumshoos." Kahuna Hala's deep voice echoed through the cave. "You have a trial goer! Do your duty and grant him his trial!"

"I'm Ash Ketchum from Pallet Town!"

Ash's voice sounded small after Hala's announcement. "I'm asking you for a battle!"

"I can hear something," Rotom Dex said. Ash and Pikachu looked around, wary.

Two Pokémon appeared from the large tunnels on the higher level.

"Are they Totem Pokémon?" Ash asked. While they had sharp teeth and appeared to be fast and strong, they were not especially large.

"No, Ash, they are not," Hala said. "They're the Totem Pokémon's allies. You'll still have to battle them, however. We shall now begin the Pokémon battles that make up this trial!"

Ash sighed. While he would have to battle the two Pokémon before him, it would only be the first round. The Totem Pokémon would come later. "Is there any data?" Ash asked Rotom.

"But of course!" Rotom answered. "Yungoos, the Loitering Pokémon. And Gumshoos, the Stakeout Pokémon. Both are Normal-types. Yungoos have sturdy fangs and jaws and when they evolve into Gumshoos, they gain a certain tenacity and patience."

Ash listened closely. "In that case, Pikachu, I choose you!" he shouted.

Pikachu strode into position.

"You, too, Rowlet!"

Rowlet bounced out of its Poké Ball and onto … the ground.

"It's asleep!" Rotom observed.

Sure enough, Rowlet was snoring. Ash charged forward. "Wake up!" he cried. Rowlet's eyes popped open. The other two Pokémon were already threatening.

"All right, Pikachu, Thunderbolt, let's go!" Ash instructed. "Rowlet, use Tackle!"

The battle was fast and furious. Both sides were fighting well. Gumshoos used Sand Attack on Pikachu. Yungoos went after Rowlet, who tried to dive away from a dirt blast.

With bursts of power shooting back and forth, the battle continued. Yungoos and Gumshoos created clouds of dust with their moves, making it hard for Ash's team to see. When they came at Pikachu and Rowlet with a double Hyper Fang Attack, Ash directed his partners to dodge it.

"You're not the only ones who can hide in your moves," Ash called out as Rowlet let off a whirlwind of glowing-green Leafage that spun around its opponents. "Pikachu, Iron Tail!" Ash commanded.

Then Rowlet soundlessly snuck behind

Gumshoos and Yungoos. "Yes!" Ash cried. "Rowlet, Tackle, let's go!"

Pikachu and Rowlet wore down the other two with move after move. At last, Hala announced it was over. "Yungoos and Gumshoos are unable to battle!"

The battle had been so intense, it was hard to believe that it was just the first round of Ash's trial.

A rumble filled the cavern. The sound of massive footsteps vibrated off the ground and stone walls. The footsteps were followed by a mighty roar.

Ash, Pikachu and Rowlet stood close together, nervously waiting for their next opponent.

CHAPTER 8

TOTEM POKÉMON

"There!" Hala declared. "This Gumshoos is truly a Totem Pokémon."

Ash gazed at his next opponent with amazement. "It's so big!" he exclaimed.

"Unreal!" was Rotom Dex's opinion. "This one is three times the size of the previous Gumshoos!"

Ash, Pikachu, and Rowlet were not only overwhelmed by Totem Gumshoos's size, they were soon overwhelmed by its power, too. Pikachu used Thunderbolt but Totem Gumshoos whacked it with Frustration.

"That Gumshoos's speed is immeasurable!" Rotom Dex reported.

Rowlet raced in and used Tackle to distract Gumshoos while Pikachu recovered but Gumshoos picked up a rock and thwacked Rowlet, too.

Ash raced to Rowlet's side. "Thanks a lot, Rowlet! You got Pikachu out of a jam!" he said, rubbing his partner's soft head. The brave Pokémon was stunned. "Take a rest! Return." Ash said and Rowlet disappeared inside its Poké Ball.

At once, Ash had to get his head back in the battle. He took a stance and called to

Pikachu. "Pikachu, Electro Ball!"

"Pika, pika, pika!" Pikachu focused its power and shot a mighty, pulsing Electro Ball at Totem Gumshoos but Gumshoos simply knocked the ball out of the way and returned a Sand Attack move.

"Pikachu, no!" Ash yelled, seeing his partner tumble and skid across the cave floor.

Pikachu grunted but got right back up.

Ash was determined, too. "Pikachu, use Quick Attack!"

Rotom was surprised by Ash's call. "I don't think using Quick Attack will have any effect at all," the device yelled but Pikachu was already in action.

Pikachu bounded ahead. When Totem Gumshoos sprang a Sand Attack, Ash instructed, "Pikachu, use that Sand Attack!

Now!"

Pikachu raced through the sand, using it as cover, whizzing all around and confusing Totem Gumshoos.

"Now!" Ash yelled again and Pikachu started landing Quick Attack moves again and again and again.

Once Totem Gumshoos was exhausted, Ash directed Pikachu to use Thunderbolt. Pikachu began to glow with intense energy, and it zoomed toward Totem Gumshoos.

"Pika-chuuuuuuuuu!" the little Pokémon cried.

Totem Gumshoos grunted and then toppled onto the ground with a crash.

"The trial is over! I declare that the challenger, Ash Ketchum, wins!" Kahuna Hala announced.

Ash celebrated with Pikachu and Rotom Dex, but his attention was soon drawn to Totem Gumshoos. It was still on the ground.

"Totem Gumshoos!" Ash approached the giant Pokémon.

Rotom Dex lingered behind, worried that it was unsafe, but Ash went right up to Gumshoos and leaned over it. "Totem Gumshoos, are you all right?"

Trying to get up, Totem Gumshoos pushed Ash out of the way. But with its other hand, it offered something to Ash.

"Gumshoos, gumshoos, gum," the
Totem Pokémon said solemnly.

Ash reached out. It was a Z-Crystal!

"For me?" he asked. "Really?"

"Gumshoos, shoos shoos gum," the Totem
Pokémon insisted Ash should take it.

"Wow," Ash said. "Thanks a lot."

He stared at the magical gem in his hand.

It was white with a single black swirl. That marking meant it was for the Normal-type Z-Move. "It's a Z-Crystal and it's all mine!" he cheered.

Watching the exchange, Kahuna Hala was impressed. It was very rare for a Totem Pokémon to give a challenger a Z-Crystal and he believed Ash must be a most unusual Trainer.

Even though Ash was thrilled to have earned a Z-Crystal, he hadn't forgotten what Hala had told him was the final stage of his challenge.

"Excuse me," Ash said, looking up at Totem Gumshoos. "I was wondering if you'd help us chase off all of the Rattata and Raticate."

Totem Gumshoos nodded in agreement.

Getting rid of the pesky, long-toothed, greedy Pokémon was far easier than the earlier stages of Kahuna Hala's trial. The next day, a group met Officer Jenny at an old warehouse where the Rattata and Raticate had been feasting. With the help of Totem Gumshoos and his allies, Ash and his team were able to chase all the unwanted Pokémon away.

Professor Kukui and Officer Jenny couldn't believe how easily Ash's new Pokémon friends defeated the nasty Mouse Pokémon.

"As kahuna of the island of Melemele, I'm very happy to verify that you have indeed passed the trial," Hala told Ash. "Your next step is the island's grand trial. Ash, I'm really looking forward to it and to see your Z-Move in battle with my very own eyes."

"I'm really looking forward to it, too!" Ash admitted.

Pikachu looked just as thrilled. Of course, the grand trial meant battling Kahuna Hala himself! Ash knew it would be a tremendous challenge but he was ready for it.

CHAPTER 9

GRAND TRIAL

Ash's good work with Totem Gumshoos and its allies ended up in the Melemele newspaper and he earned a certificate of appreciation from Officer Jenny. It was very exciting, but for Ash, it was all part of his journey to become a Pokémon Master.

His next big step was the grand trial and

Ash didn't want to waste any time. He planned to battle Kahuna Hala the very next day.

The grand trial included a certain amount of ceremony. Part of the ceremony was for both opponents to meditate together at a temple called the Ruins of Conflict, which was deep in the forest. Pikachu and Hala's partner, Hariyama, were there, too.

"Today we will perform a grand trial battle with our young challenger, Ash. I now ask Tapu Koko, guardian of conflict, to bestow upon us the power of Alola ... of all the islands."

"Please, Tapu Koko," Ash added. "This will be my grand trial with Kahuna Hala, so I want you to watch it!"

The two future opponents closed their

eyes and remained silent.

Ash had a hard time staying still. His arms felt stiff and his foot itched! But he tried to concentrate – for Tapu Koko. Ever since the Island Guardian had given him his first Z-Crystal, Ash had felt a bond with the mystical Pokémon. True, he wanted to one day be able to battle the powerful Pokémon again, but he also wanted to be worthy. He wanted to believe that Tapu Koko recognised something special in him.

After a while, Kahuna Hala chuckled to himself. "You can move now, Ash," he said.

"Do you think Tapu Koko heard us?" Ash asked the kahuna.

"I would say there's a good possibility Tapu Koko heard us," he replied. "But as Island Guardians go, Tapu Koko follows its own path."

At that moment, there was a shrill coo that echoed through the leafy forest. Ash was certain that their ceremony had a special guest!

After their meditation, Ash and Hala met with Professor Kukui and Rotom Dex at the outdoor battle arena. It was a simple stone battle space, without stands or fanfare, surrounded by palm trees.

"All right, Ash," Professor Kukui coached him. "One thing before your grand trial begins. Do you know the correct poses to use the Normal-type Z-Move?"

The professor's question referred to the specific Z-Crystal that Ash had received from Totem Gumshoos. It allowed him to do just one of several kinds of Z-Moves.

"I sure do!" Ash assured his teacher. "We practised till it's second nature. Right,

Pikachu?"

"Pika, pika!" Pikachu agreed.

"Yes, he is correct," responded Rotom Dex.

"Way to lock on and master your Z-Move!" the professor said.

"I can't wait to use it!" Ash replied.

"When you use your Z-Move," Professor Kukui advised, "both you and your Pokémon expend a large amount of energy. So with

the way you, Pikachu and Rowlet are now, your Z-Move should be quite tiring."

Ash listened closely. "The important thing is when I use it, is that right?" he confirmed.

"Exactly, Ash," Professor Kukui said. "We're ready, Hala!"

"It's truly an honour to battle you!" Ash and Kahuna Hala said at once. Then the grand trial began!

"Ready to go, Rowlet?" Ash asked. "I choose you!"

Rotom Dex was certain Rowlet would be asleep when it appeared from the Poké Ball. But Rowlet was wide awake and ready to battle.

"Crabrawler, come out!" Hala said, summoning his first Pokémon. Crabrawler was a low-to-the-ground Pokémon with four legs and two mighty pincers.

"Crabrawler?" Ash questioned. "Rotom?"

"My greatest pleasure," Rotom replied, pulling up the data. "Crabrawler, the Boxing Pokémon. A Fighting-type. Crabrawler is always aiming to be number one. It will guard its weak spots with its claws in battle and throw punches while looking for an opening. Since Rowlet is a Flying-type, it's a good match for our side!"

"Great!" Ash replied, preparing himself.

At once, Hala called his first shot. "Crabrawler, use Bubble Beam!"

Ash asked Rowlet to dodge and then use Peck. Rowlet's first moves proved successful but Kahuna Hala soon picked up on Ash and Rowlet's tactics and countered them well. Crabrawler used its strong, sharp claws to grab Rowlet mid-attack. Then, with Brutal Swing, Crabrawler could swing

Rowlet around and around and fling the other Pokémon high in the sky, nearly stunning it.

As the fight went on, Crabrawler's attack power only increased.

"That one's strong," Ash mumbled after Rowlet's Leafage move didn't do any damage to Crabrawler at all.

"I think you know by now that my Pokémon are trained far beyond what you're used to, my young Ash," Kahuna Hala declared.

Watching, Professor Kukui had to agree. Kahuna Hala's Pokémon were trained to the top of their abilities.

Ash felt bewildered. What could he do? What move might catch Hala and his mighty Crabrawler off guard?

Just then, Rowlet fluttered down near

Ash's shoulder, surprising him. "Ah! Stop!" Ash cried. "You're always showing up that way and I have no clue ..."

Ash suddenly stopped and smiled at Rowlet. His stealthy Pokémon had helped him come up with a plan!

"Okay, Rowlet," Ash told his teammate quietly. "You're going to use Leafage one more time, but you'll scare Crabrawler when you do it!"

Rowlet seemed to understand at once. It released Leafage as soon as it started to dive toward Crabrawler. The glowing green leaves swirled around in a forceful wind, aimed right at Crabrawler.

Hala watched, confused about why Ash would try the same move again. He called for the attack that had been so successful against Leafage last time. "Crabrawler,

Bubble Beam!" he called.

Crabrawler's move hit Leafage head-on, creating a giant, hazy cloud. But when the cloud cleared away, Crabrawler could not find Rowlet.

Rowlet had sneaked up right behind him and Ash ordered Peck, Peck and more Peck!

Rowlet's attacks were working. Crabrawler was too exhausted to dodge.

"Now that's effective!" Rotom Dex

cheered.

Hala ordered a Power-Up Punch. "Crabrawler, grab Rowlet and use Brutal Swing!"

"Be careful, Rowlet!" Ash advised. "Tackle, let's go!"

At the exact moment that Crabrawler lifted its claw, letting down its guard, Rowlet aimed a Tackle that sent the Fighting-type Pokémon flying. Crabrawler landed with a thud.

Professor Kukui rushed over to check on Crabrawler's condition. "Crabrawler is unable to battle!" he called out.

But the battle was still far from over.

CHAPTER 10

FINAL BATTLE

Kahuna Hala returned Crabrawler to its Poké Ball. "You battled valiantly," he told his teammate. Then he readied himself for the remainder of the grand trial.

Back on Ash's side of the arena, they were having a small celebration when Rotom Dex realised that Rowlet had fallen asleep.

Ash tried to wake his teammate but it was no use. It was exhausted from its strong showing in the battle with Crabrawler.

Ash sighed and got out Rowlet's Poké Ball. "Rowlet, you really did an awesome job, but we can take it from here."

After Rowlet was safely returned, Ash looked to Pikachu. Kahuna Hala had already tapped Hariyama as his next Pokémon.

Rotom Dex shared the data. "Hariyama, the Arm Thrust Pokémon, a Fighting-type. Hariyama's impressive bulk is actually all muscle. When its muscles are flexed, they are hard as a rock. It is said that one hit from a Hariyama can send a ten-ton truck flying."

"I'm counting on you, buddy," Ash told Pikachu as his partner jumped up on his shoulder. "I choose you!"

Pikachu pounced to the ground as Hariyama grunted a challenge.

Hariyama easily deflected Pikachu's first move of Iron Tail with Fake Out, followed quickly by Knock Off. Rotom and Professor Kukui agreed that it was a smart move combination.

Pikachu was determined but Electro Ball didn't do a thing. Hariyama countered with Arm Thrust and then kept throwing thrusts, batting Pikachu back and forth.

Pikachu took a huge amount of damage. Even when it slipped by Hariyama and landed a direct hit with Thunderbolt, the move had no effect.

Ash knew his only remaining move was the Z-Move, but he also knew he needed to choose the right time to use it.

On the other end of the arena, Kahuna Hala had decided it was his and Hariyama's time.

Hala called for Belly Drum, a move that maximises a Pokémon's strength but uses up a lot of stamina. Then he belted out, "Here we go … do it!"

At once, Hala and Hariyama began to make the same graceful but powerful moves, sliding their legs in the air, stomping their feet and flexing their arms.

"Is that … a Z-Move?" Ash asked out loud.

"Correct," declared Hala. "I make the wills of myself, Melemele and Tapu Koko as one." He paused and took a deep breath. Then he and Hariyama began throwing fiery punches. "I … am … the … ka–hu–na! This is the moment when our strengths become one!"

"Pikachu, use Quick Attack!" Ash directed. "Dodge that Z-Move."

"Pika!" Pikachu ran straight at Hariyama.

"All-Out Pummeling!" Hala commanded. "Let's go!"

Pikachu ran head-on, dodging the constant attacks from Hariyama. But its final blast landed, sending Pikachu tumbling.

Luckily, Pikachu recovered quickly. Ash knew he needed to deal some damage, so

he devised a combination attack. "Pikachu! Quick Attack! One more time!"

This time, Pikachu circled around and around Hariyama, confusing the much larger Pokémon. "Now use Iron Tail!"

When Pikachu zapped Hariyama's ankle, the Arm Thrust Pokémon dropped to its knees.

"Hariyama took damage from that!" Rotom Dex announced.

"Well, I guess it took a combination to fight a combination," Professor Kukui noted.

"Great job, Pikachu!" Ash cheered. At that moment, he knew the time had come. "Now it's our turn!"

Ash and Pikachu both crossed their arms, and electric pulses began to crackle around them. Ash's Z-Ring glowed with power. The two began their sequence of moves that drew from the mystical energy of the ring.

"It's happening. Pikachu and I are becoming one and that's making us much stronger than either one of us!" Ash cried. "Here we go! Full power, now!"

Pikachu took off like a bolt, leaving smoke in its trail. "Breakneck Blitz!" Ash cried. Hariyama had no time to get out of the way.

"Pika pi pi pi pi pi pi pi pi!" Pikachu came at it like a comet, a bright centre with a tail of flame. It was a direct hit!

"That was awesome, Pikachu! We used a Z-Move!" Ash could hardly believe it!

Professor Kukui assessed the damage to their opponent. "Melemele Kahuna Hala's Hariyama is unable to battle!" he said. "Which means the winner of this Melemele grand trial is the challenger, Ash Ketchum!"

"Ash wins the trial. Hooray!" Rotom celebrated.

Kahuna Hala thanked Hariyama as he returned the Pokémon to its Poké Ball. Then he turned to Ash. "I thoroughly enjoyed our splendid battle, young Ash. You and Rowlet and Pikachu gave it everything you had."

"Thank you very much, sir," Ash replied.

"Pika pika chu!" cheered Pikachu.

"As far as your Z-Move?" Hala continued. "It overflowed with the joy of accomplishment. I marveled at feeling your youthful, yet experienced, aura."

Ash smiled. The kahuna liked to speak in flowery language but Ash could tell it was a supreme compliment.

"So, as the Melemele Island Kahuna, I hereby proclaim that Ash Ketchum has passed the grand trial!"

"All right!" Ash exclaimed with a clenched fist.

"Good for you," the kahuna said. "But please don't forget to take this." Then he held out his hand and Ash caught a glimpse of a Z-Crystal. "It's your Fightinium Z. With this Z-Crystal, you'll be able to use the Fighting-type Z-Move."

"Awesome! Thank you!" Ash replied.

But before he could take the Z-Crystal, a high call trilled over the trees and there was a rush of wind that whooshed all around.

"What was that?" Ash wondered.

"Could that have been ... Tapu Koko?" Professor Kukui said.

"It was so fast, I have no data," Rotom Dex stated.

When Kahuna Hala looked back at the

crystal in his hand, it had changed! "It can't be!" he said.

"An Electrium Z?" Ash said, looking at the gem. "That looks just like the one I got from Tapu Koko!"

"Fascinating!" Hala exclaimed. "In all of my experience, this is the first time Tapu Koko has taken so much interest in a challenger. Eventually, I'll learn why. For now, I believe that this Electrium Z belongs

to you. Take this Z-Crystal and use it with wisdom!"

"I will," Ash promised. "This Z-Crystal is all mine! An Electrium Z!"

That night, Kahuna Hala hosted a grand celebration for Ash and his friends from the Pokémon School. After all, without their help, Ash might not have learned the secret to banishing the Rattata and Raticate. That had been just one stage of his Island Challenge. Each accomplishment had been part of the adventure. And with each step, Ash was discovering more about all he would learn on his journey to becoming a Pokémon Master!

FIND OUT HOW ASH AND FRIENDS'
ADVENTURES ON ALOLA BEGAN IN

THE POKÉMON SCHOOL

READ ON FOR A SNEAK PEAK ...

"Yippee! Whoo!" Ash yelled. "AWESOME!"

Ash grinned as he gazed out at the wide, blue ocean. He felt a splash of water on his face. Melemele Island, one of several islands in the Alola region, was the perfect place for a holiday! He had Pikachu, his best friend and beloved Pokémon, on his shoulder. The island sun was warm and bright. What could be better?

The answer: zipping over the waves while riding a super cool Sharpedo! Sharpedo was the famous Alola Pokémon jet ski. Instead of a machine with a motor, it was a fabulous Water- and Dark-type Pokémon with super speed.

"Full throttle, Sharpedo!" Ash directed. With several strong flips of its powerful tail, Sharpedo zoomed ahead.

This thrilling Sharpedo ride was just one of the amazing activities Ash could enjoy on Melemele Island. The Alola region was a tropical paradise, and it had all kinds of unique Pokémon. Even though Ash and his mum were on holiday, he was still thinking about Pokémon.

Ash loved nothing more than encountering new Pokémon. It was his goal to become a Pokémon Master. He had travelled to many regions on his quest to compete at top Pokémon Gyms, but he already knew that his time in Alola would be special.

While Ash and his mum were on
Melemele Island, they had an important
task. Professor Oak, the famous Pokémon
Professor who lived in Ash's hometown
in the Kanto region, had asked them for
a favour. Professor Oak needed them
to deliver a Pokémon Egg to his cousin,
Samson Oak. It was a mysterious Egg, and
Ash knew it was a very important job.

To get to Samson Oak, Ash and his mum
took a taxi. But it wasn't just any taxi.

"My first Pokémon taxi!" Ash declared
from the comfortable seat of a cart pulled
by a strong Tauros. "This is the best EVER!"

Ash was thrilled. Pikachu made a happy
squeak, and the Tauros replied with a
friendly grunt. Also along for the trip
was Mr. Mime, Ash's mum's Pokémon

companion. Mr. Mime, a Psychic- and Fairy-type Pokémon, had actually won the tickets for their big island getaway!

"Here in the Alola region, we use the power of Pokémon to go anywhere and everywhere," the taxi driver explained. "We refer to these Pokémon as Ride Pokémon. When you travel on land, you take a Land Ride Pokémon. When you want to fly, you take an Air Ride Pokémon. On water, a Water Ride Pokémon."

Ash found it all fascinating. He loved learning new Pokémon facts!

His mum was more interested in the exotic fruit at the local market. She wanted to buy some berries, so the taxi driver pulled Tauros to a stop.

As Ash got out of the cart, he noticed something out of the corner of his eye. It wasn't fruit.

"It's a Pokémon," Ash murmured, rushing over to investigate. The Pokémon was halfway underground, with its tan-and-orange striped head poking out. "So cool! I wonder what its name is?"

Ash leaned down, and the Pokémon reached out and pinched his nose with its strong pincer-like jaws.

As soon as the Bug-type Pokémon let go, it dove underground and dug an escape tunnel. "OK, let's catch it, Pikachu!" Ash cried, holding his sore nose.

In an instant, the two friends had rushed off into a nearby forest, leaving the market – and Ash's mum – far behind. They raced after the speedy Pokémon.

However, once they were deep in the forest, the Pokémon had too many places to hide. Tall, leafy trees rose high overhead, and lush plants grew all over the forest floor.

"Guess we missed it," Ash said, panting to catch his breath. Ash looked up and realised that he didn't know where he was. He thought about his mum. "Where were we supposed to take that Egg again?"

READ THE POKÉMON SCHOOL TO
FIND OUT WHAT HAPPENS NEXT!

WHICH POKÉMON DID YOU FIND IN THIS ADVENTURE?

☐ LITTEN

☐ STOUTLAND

☐ CRABRAWLER

Find information on lots of Pokémon
in the Official Pokémon Encyclopedia!

LOOK OUT FOR THESE OTHER OFFICIAL POKÉMON BOOKS